This book is ESPECIALLY for Isla and Darcy.
I hope you both enjoy it!

BLOOMSBURY CHILDREN'S BOOKS
Bloomsbury Publishing Plc
50 Bedford Square, London WC1B 3DP, UK
29 Earlsfort Terrace, Dublin 2, Ireland

BLOOMSBURY, BLOOMSBURY CHILDREN'S BOOKS and the Diana logo
are trademarks of Bloomsbury Publishing Plc

First published in Great Britain in 2023 by Bloomsbury Publishing Plc

A catalogue record for this book is available from the British Library

ISBN HB: 978 1 5266 4246 2
ISBN PB: 978 1 5266 4247 9
ISBN eBook: 978 1 5266 4245 5

1 3 5 7 9 10 8 6 4 2

Printed and bound in China by Leo Paper Products, Heshan, Guangdong

MIX
Paper from
responsible sources
FSC
www.fsc.org   FSC® C020056

To find out more about our authors and books visit www.bloomsbury.com and sign up for our newsletters

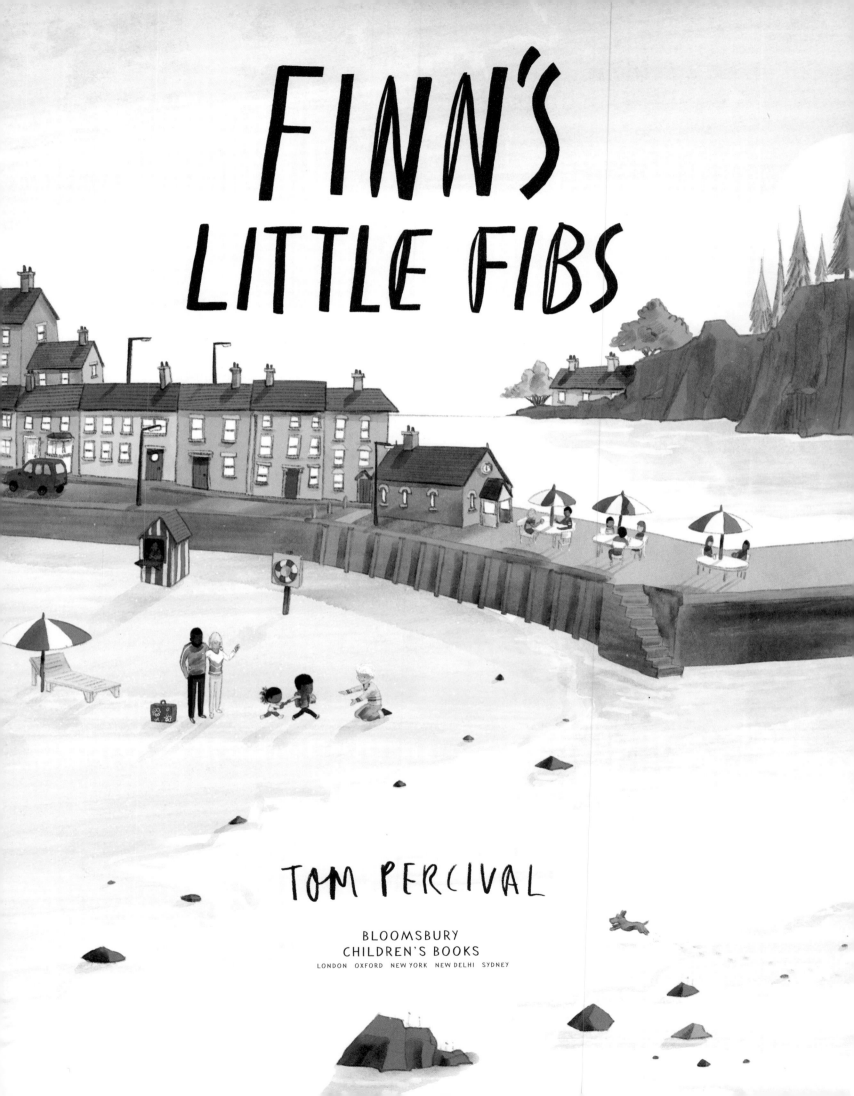

FINN'S LITTLE FIBS

TOM PERCIVAL

BLOOMSBURY
CHILDREN'S BOOKS
LONDON OXFORD NEW YORK NEW DELHI SYDNEY

Finn was *buzzing*
with excitement!

He was spending a few days at Grandma's house with his sister, Simone.

Finn *loved* staying there . . .

Grandma always bought them treats . . .

She took them to eat fish and chips on the beach.

And she let Finn stay up a *whole*
half hour later than usual.

It was *brilliant!*

Grandma's house was filled with
all sorts of wonderful, beautiful
but VERY fragile things.

Finn was usually *extremely* careful in Grandma's house,
but today he was a bit over-excited.

He bounced his
ball higher . . .

and
higher . . .

and *higher*,
until . . .

Finn stared at the broken
clock in horror.

He tried his best to fix it.

But it didn't *really* work.

Then Grandma walked in.
She looked at the mess.
She looked at Finn.

His tummy twisted, his mind **raced**,
and *that* was when it happened . . .

Finn told a fib!

"Simone broke
the clock," he said.
"I was trying to fix it."

It wasn't a *big* fib. It could *easily* have happened.
But as soon as he said it . . .

A strange little blob appeared.

Grandma didn't notice the blob, but she *did*
ask how Simone had reached the clock.

Finn panicked and told ANOTHER fib!

Immediately, a **second** blob appeared.

Grandma didn't notice this one either –
but she *did* look very sad about her clock.

It made Finn feel funny inside.

The next day, Mum and Dad phoned.
After they'd spoken with Grandma,
they asked Finn about the clock.

Somehow, *another* fib slipped out . . .

And a THIRD blob appeared.

Now that he'd started fibbing, it felt *impossible* to stop!

All weekend long, the fibs about the clock
piled up around him.

Finn couldn't snuggle on the sofa because
the fibs **all got in the way.**

He didn't want to play with Simone
because the fibs made him sad.

And he couldn't eat any fish and chips
because the fibs made his tummy feel strange.

Finn felt awful!

If *only* he'd never told that first fib. But he HAD –
and it was too late to change that now.
Or *was* it?

There was one thing he could do . . .

He could tell the truth.

Finn's face grew hot.
What if Grandma got cross?

But he knew what
he had to do . . .

"It was *me*!" said Finn suddenly, the words tripping over themselves. "I broke the clock. I'm really SORRY I blamed Simone."

Finn heard a soft, quiet *whsssssssssh* . . .

And one by one, the whole crowd
of fibs VANISHED!

Finn felt so much lighter!

"Don't worry, Finn," said Grandma.
"We *all* make mistakes
sometimes . . .

Well done for telling
the truth."

After that, everything was back to normal.
In fact, it was *better* than normal . . .

It was the BEST holiday *ever!*

From that day on, Finn decided
he would always try to tell
the TRUTH . . .

And if, by mistake, a fib ever did pop out,
as they *sometimes* do, then he
owned up right away!